G

The Long Pony Trek

 The

Alfred A. Knopf　New York

Long Pony Trek

Rolf Lengstrand & Pierre L. Rolén

Photographs by Lennart Blomqvist
Translated by Marianne Turner

Photographs by Lennart Blomqvist, and acknowledgements to Olle Hagelroth, C. J. Lewenhaupt, Arthur Svenonius, Ola Lager, Rolf Lengstrand, Pierre Rolén, Heinz von Sterneck. Also to "Bunty" Douglas for technical help received with the translation.

Originally published in Stockholm, Sweden by B. Wahlströms Bokförlag AB as PONNY KLUBBEN GENOM ROK OCH ELD, © 1964 by Rolf Lengstrand and Pierre L. Rolén. Published in Great Britain by Brockhampton Press, Ltd. © 1966 by Brockhampton Press, Ltd.

The Long Pony Trek

The heat was oppressive. Not a drop of rain had fallen for a long time, and the grass in the great pastures had turned yellow. It was the driest summer anyone could remember.

Several girls had tethered their ponies on the hill behind the old railway station. The ponies stood, switching their tails, and now and then taking a bite from the dry grass.

In the forest on the other side of the valley, the railway track ran like two silver lines towards the red station building. It wasn't often that the train stopped here, but today was an exception.

The girls sat silent, waiting.

Then came the expected signal.

In the distance, from the edge of the forest, they heard a shrill whistle. The ponies raised their heads and pricked up their ears.

"It's coming!"

"What if she's missed it?"

"She can't have. She's going to lead the pony trek tomorrow."

It wasn't until the train was moving off and the last compartment had passed that the solitary figure of a girl could be seen on the platform.

She looked around, puzzled. This wasn't what she had expected. Why was there no one to meet her?

She threw her saddlebags over her shoulder and went around the corner of the station building onto the road.

There she came to a standstill. She could hear the beat of hoofs and the happy shrieks of girls. Her face lit up as she turned around and saw a troop of ponies with flowing manes and tails come clattering over the old wooden bridge toward her.

"Hello, Fia, nice to see you!" called the girl in front as she reined in her pony.

Fia was surrounded. The ponies nickered a greeting to her while the girls talked excitedly.

"I thought perhaps you'd forgotten I was coming. After all, George promised. . ."

"Oh, yes, but he couldn't get away."

"The pony trek starts tomorrow morning, early," added one of the other girls. "We brought a spare pony for you to ride home."

Fia looked around eagerly and asked, "Tiny?"

But she couldn't see her favorite pony anywhere.

"Hurry up, Fia. Come and hold Pontus. He's getting restless!" called Karin from the bridge.

Fia went over and gently stroked Pontus' neck. Then she adjusted the girth, which was twisted.

"He's more comfortable now," she said, and smiled at Karin. She let down the stirrup straps, put her foot in the stirrup, and swung into the saddle.

"Why didn't you bring Tiny?" she asked.

It was Karin who answered, "He's not very well."

Fia was stunned. In silence the girls started off along the winding path leading to the stream. There they stopped and let the ponies graze for a short time.

"Let's follow the stream. It's easier to get across farther down," called Eva. Then she caught her breath. "But look!" she exclaimed.

The girls turned their heads in the direction Eva was pointing.

Above, on the hillside, roamed a large herd of shiny ponies. There were bays and roans, blacks and chestnuts . . . and there were skittish foals, ready to take part in everything, though not straying far from their mothers.

"They belong to us," shouted Karin excitedly.

Everyone was thrilled at the sight.

"What a lot of new foals! And look! Lightning is the leader again this year!"

"It's amazing that you can see that from this distance, Fia!" exclaimed Karin, with admiration in her voice.

The girls stayed for some time, watching the herd continue slowly on its way.

"We must get started now." It was Eva who spoke. "We're still two miles from home."

"And dinner is in an hour," said Karin, closing her legs on Benito's sides.

Fia had spent a whole long autumn and an even longer winter living for the day when she would be back at Lakeholme Stud Farm. She knew she was welcome there. In George's last letter there was a message from his father who ran the farm. It said, "P.S. We look foward to seeing you, Fia," and it was signed "The Captain." And now, very soon, she would be seeing Tiny again. It was nearly a year since she saw him last. That was when, together, they had won The Long Pony Race.

She smiled as she thought of how it had all begun, when Tiny was just a newborn foal and she had practically lived in his stall.

"Whew, it's hot!" groaned Karin, rousing Fia out of her thoughts.

"It certainly is," she agreed, removing her sweater.

Then something unexpected happened.

Pontus squealed and swung sharply around. Fia was taken by surprise, but she managed to steady the horse just as a majestic shape moved smoothly across the path. It was a large elk.

"Look out!" she cried to Karin.

But Fia's warning was too late. She saw Benito rear, and Karin clutch the saddle. The next moment Karin slipped backwards and fell to the ground.

"Don't let go of the reins!" cried Fia.

Karin stood up. Brushing herself and straightening her cap, she looked after the disappearing elk. Proudly, she held up her hand which was still firmly holding the reins.

She patted Benito and mounted again.

The girls trotted out of the forest. From the south gate the path took them the last short distance to Lakeholme Farm.

"There you are at last!" called one of the girls who had walked out to meet them.

When the gate shut behind Fia she felt she had come home. She rode down the path where the foliage was so thick that it formed a green roof over her head. Everything was just the same. She continued past the low stable buildings and turned off into the shadow of the tall doorway.

In the yard stood George. "Hello, Fia!" he said and smiled.

George held Pontus while Fia dismounted. "Hello, George. How's Tiny?"

"I knew that would be the first thing you'd ask. I don't think there's a lot to worry about, but he seems out of sorts. I've asked the veterinarian to come tomorrow."

"Where is he now?" Fia asked.

"In the enclosure behind the stable. But first of all you must come into the house. We're going to eat, and then Father wants to talk to us."

After dinner they all assembled in the tack room. There was complete silence when the Captain began to speak, "All of you, especially those of you who are new to the pony club, listen carefully. The trekking begins tomorrow morning at seven. George," the Captain pointed his riding whip at his son, "you will be responsible for the ponies. Fia, you will be responsible for the girls. You will stay overnight on farms, but the last night you will sleep in the open. Take good care of the horses! You will be away for a number of days, and you have a long way to go."

There was a ghost of a smile as he looked at the group of girls who were listening so attentively. "Best of luck!" he ended.

Fia turned to George. "I'm going to the paddock," she said.

She followed the path past the stable and looked around the paddock. There stood Tiny!

Fia saw at once that he was not himself. She remembered him quite differently . . . the proud carriage, the slim body, and the smooth, supple legs; the shiny neck, strong mane, and sweeping tail.

Now he stood there by the gate with drooping head, pawing nervously.

"Tiny!" she said softly.

He turned and nodded his head.

Fia went up to him and put her cheek against his nose. "Don't worry, Tiny, I'm here. Tomorrow the veterinarian will come, and he will make you better. You can't imagine how much I've missed you!"

Then Fia did something she was to regret later. She did it, although she ought to have known better. She went into the stable and got his saddle and bridle. "We'll just take a little walk. You'd like that, wouldn't you?"

Fia mounted. Very slowly and carefully she rode up the hill and down toward the lake.

She could tell that Tiny was listless. He walked stiffly, and his muscles trembled.

Fia turned and took the short cut over the fields back to the paddock.

Before leaving Tiny, Fia gave him a hug. He looked at her with big, lusterless eyes.

"See you tomorrow," she whispered.

She hurried up the slope. Tiny stayed where he was without moving, following her with his eyes until she disappeared over the hill.

Next morning, everyone was up early. The trek would start in less than an hour. Fia came walking across the stable yard.

"Fia! The veterinarian's arrived," Karin called, "and I think Tiny has made a pig of himself."

Fia went into the stable with Karin following her.

The veterinarian was examining Tiny's feet. He picked up one at a time and pinched it with a pair of pincers. Tiny snatched back his leg as though it hurt.

"Just as I thought," said the veterinarian to George. "One of the girls must have turned him out on rich pasture." He pointed to the pony's hot feet. Fia glanced quickly at Karin.

"How is he?" she asked the veterinarian anxiously.

"He's got a temperature and his hoofs are painful."

"Is it dangerous?" exclaimed Karin, alarmed.

"It could be worse."

The veterinarian gave Tiny an injection in his leg. "I think he'll be all right now," he said, "if you make sure he has nothing rich to eat for twenty-four hours and is only allowed to walk where the ground is soft."

"I'll take him to the paddock in the woods," said George. "There's hardly any grass there, and the ground is soft."

"That's good." The veterinarian collected his instruments. "I must go to the blacksmith and ask him to trim Tiny's hoofs." In the stable doorway he turned. "There's just one more thing! Make sure none of the girls gets the absurd idea of riding him."

Fia could feel herself turning red. How could she have been so stupid?

"How did you know that Tiny had overeaten?" asked Fia, when she and Karin were alone again.

Karin gave Fia an anxious look of embarrassment. "I forgot to fasten the lock on Tiny's box, and when I got back he had escaped. Promise not to tell anyone . . . I didn't mean to do it."

Fia promised.

She went toward the main building where the girls were standing, all ready to start. She felt a pang as she passed the rack where Tiny's saddle hung.

So the pony trek began.

The sun glowed on the light summer clouds which slowly drifted across the blue sky.

The young riders were on their way!

This was the hour which the girls had looked forward to eagerly, which they had dreamed of for months: to go on a real pony trek; to ride through the countryside in summer clothes; to follow new, unknown paths . . . and, best of all, for a few days to be one with your pony, and to be able to call it your own . . .

The ponies' hoofs padded softly on the springy woodland path, making last year's dry leaves rustle. They followed the main road in small whirling clouds of dust and clattered over the bridge. Some kingfishers, which had been diving for food, took flight in alarm and with rapid beats of their wings flew away over the lily pads.

So the cavalcade turned into the forest.

Twice they halted, and each time the girls attended first to their ponies, before they started hungrily on their sandwiches.

It turned out to be a wonderful day!

Yet they were quite pleased when, toward evening, they spotted the farm where they were to stay the night.

"We've made it!" called George. "Get unsaddled and see the ponies are watered before they're groomed."

He was responsible for the ponies. He rode down to the paddock and examined the barbed-wire fence for holes. Then he rode back and inspected the ponies, felt their quarters and legs to discover any possible injury. Everything was in order.

Fia divided up the work among the girls.

She, herself, worked tirelessly. She supervised everything. But she couldn't stop thinking about Tiny.

Karin saw Fia leading Pontus to the trough filled with fresh water, and she noticed that Fia looked worried.

"Fia, it won't be long before Tiny is well."

Fia looked up. She smiled at Karin, who winked at her.

The girls' turn came when the ponies were groomed and fed.

On the shore of the lake, the air was filled with happy laughter. They could now enjoy wading out into its refreshing water.

"The world's best bathtub!" said Karin with a laugh, and began to soap herself.

Fia let Pontus wade out into the lake. Another girl followed her example. The ponies, too, enjoyed it. They whinnied and snorted and, once they were back on the shore, their bodies glistened in the evening sun.

At the farm someone was sounding a bell. "Dinner! Come and get it."

Before a minute had passed, the shore was deserted.

The days went by, and the ties of friendship between the girls and ponies grew ever stronger. The exciting ride had continued through shady forests, across fields and meadows, along winding paths, and up on to high ridges.

Fia was very pleased. So far, everything had worked out well.

By now they had reached Dalby Farm, where the girls were to spend the night and all the next day.

It was bedtime. Fia opened the window and breathed in all the scents of the summer evening. The sky was cloudless, but it had changed color.

"I think the good weather will continue," she said to herself.

George was up early. He had already been down to the paddock, and now he came riding across the open space in front of the house.

"Where's Fia?" he asked.

"She went with the 'stagecoach'," replied one of the girls with a yawn, and continued to tie her shoelaces.

The "stagecoach" was one of the old carriages on the farm, and only used when Sophie, the daughter of the house, went to the station to meet someone.

"They're coming," cried Karin, who had stationed herself by the gate.

Now the carriage came rattling across the courtyard with Fia as escort. It swung around the circular lawn and stopped in front of the door. Everyone burst out laughing. In the coachman's seat Sophie sat like a queen—on her head was a cap that might have come straight out of a Wild West movie.

In the back was Christine.

"Don't look at me," shouted Christine as she jumped down from the carriage in a dress. Quickly she snatched her bag and rushed off into the house. Like a whirlwind she was back again, in jeans and a checked shirt, calling as she leaped over the porch rail.

"Hey!" she cried, "I've got a surprise for you! Everyone in the pony trek is invited to The Great Pony Day, the pony field trials at Stromsberg tomorrow."

All the girls began making happy plans.

"Where's my pony?" asked Christine, running toward the enclosure.

"Christine's here! Christine's here!" they all shouted.

Some of the girls, who were already out exercising their ponies, heard the shouts. They turned around at once and rode back to the farm.

"Who's Christine?" asked one of the new girls.

Fia smiled. "She's a friend of Sophie's and spends all the time she can here. She has her own way of riding and schooling ponies."

"Yes, it's going to be a real circus now," said Karin. "Just look over there!"

In the paddock stood Christine, feeding one of the foals with sugar— in her own special way!

"We must start half an hour earlier tomorrow morning to get to Stromsberg in time," said George, when the girls had quieted down. "One of the club members, Madeleine, will be competing, so it'll be espe- cially exciting."

"What do they mean by pony field trials?" someone asked.

"There are three separate events," explained George. "Schooling, cross- country riding, and jumping."

Another day dawned, The Great Pony Day. The sun rose like a red balloon behind the forest. There wasn't a breath of wind, and a light mist veiled the countryside.

Sophie stood waving in the courtyard as the girls departed, heading toward the bottom of the valley.

Christine said good-by to her favorite foal, then she, too, leaped into her saddle and caught up with the others.

The atmosphere at the Stromsberg racing stable was tense. Girths and bits were being checked for the day's events. The schooling trials had been carried out yesterday, and today riders and ponies were again to be put to the test.

Cross-country riding and jumping were the events scheduled.

One girl remained, sitting by herself in the tack room. She was trying to conquer the nervous tension which always came on her just before a trial. She was playing with one of the kittens which belonged to the stable cat.

"Madeleine, you must get ready!"

Again there were butterflies in her stomach. It was too bad that Blue Sham had hurt his leg while being transported here. Nothing serious . . . but enough to make him miss a few valuable points in the schooling test.

He was all right today and, if nothing unforeseen happened, he would still stand a good chance—if only he managed the water jump. In the dip halfway down the course was rather a steep slope. It didn't look difficult, but Madeleine was afraid of it.

"Promise to keep your paws crossed for me," she said to the kitten, who purred in reply.

She got ready and went into the stable where Blue Sham was waiting for her in his stall.

Madeleine led him toward the starting point for the cross-country trial. She patted his neck.

"Now it's our turn—yours and mine," she said, as she pulled the strap of her crash cap tight. She put her foot into the stirrup and swung into the saddle. Blue Sham quivered eagerly as she gathered up the reins.

Starter's orders!

Madeleine settled in the saddle as Blue Sham made a swift getaway. His hoofs drummed against the ground. Madeleine shortened the reins, and Blue Sham followed the track as it turned sharply to the left. He snorted and increased his speed.

The hard ground, scored by many hoofprints, seemed to fly past.

"Careful! Mind your legs," she said, urging him on, trying to keep her voice calm.

They turned in among the trees. Here on the woodland path the ground was softer. Madeleine bent forward in the saddle to avoid being hit in the face by overhanging branches.

Blue Sham hurtled toward the first obstacle.

Madeleine judged the distance for the takeoff. She drove on, and Blue Sham made no mistakes. He gracefully and easily took the jump with his tail flowing. Madeleine found time to give him a grateful pat.

At a full gallop they swept downhill. Blue Sham was putting all his energy into the long strides by which so much would be gained. Madeleine was all attention. Down the slope they went. Now came the real test. Madeleine took a deep breath: this was their hardest obstacle.

The water jump was just below them! Madeleine shortened the reins slightly. Then came the jump. Blue Sham flew over and landed with a good margin on the other side. Madeleine was surprised at how easily he had managed it. Then they rode uphill again, through the woods and into the field. The rows of spectators flashed past. Someone was calling her name, but Madeleine never knew who it was. She and Blue Sham had more important things to think about.

Her heart jumped into her throat! She thought Blue Sham was about to fall . . . but, judging by his frantic speed, there couldn't be much to worry about. They swept around the gray barn and flew at top speed toward the big jump.

The logs seemed to Madeleine to be rushing toward her. Blue Sham took the jump—perhaps a few feet too soon, but he cleared it easily. On and on they went, uphill and downhill, over obstacles, some easy, some difficult, then on to the last straight stretch. Madeleine felt indescribably happy when Blue Sham increased his speed and, amidst cheering from the spectators, made a frantic spurt toward the finish.

Now there was only the track jumping left. George, Fia, and the girls were sitting in the grandstand, watching the contest with rapt attention.

Now it was Madeleine's turn. She had changed into her riding jacket. Neither she nor Blue Sham made any mistakes.

"Today she seems unbeatable," said George with admiration. "Just look at the easy way she and Blue Sham take the obstacles."

"I only hope it goes on like this."

Suddenly all the spectators held their breath as they heard Blue Sham hit a bar. Despairingly, Madeleine turned and looked back. The bar swayed for a moment . . . but it stayed in position.

"That was close." George breathed a sigh of relief.

The last obstacle: Madeleine and Blue Sham appeared to fly over it and crossed the finishing line without losing a single point.

Now came the presentation of prizes. The riders stood in a row in front of the grandstand.

"The winner of the Pony Field Trials . . ."

Madeleine sat motionless on her pony in her jet-black riding jacket and gleaming white shirt. Blue Sham held his head high, and the wind played with his mane, making it look like a plume of victory. The murmur of the spectators had died down. All you could hear was the slapping sound of flags.

Madeleine calmly raised her whip to her helmet, saluting. She had won . . . This was a great moment . . .

"Come along, let's go and congratulate her!"

George stepped into the enclosure, and Fia followed him on to the grass.

"Hello, Madeleine! You did very well! Here's Fia."

"Congratulations!"

Fia looked at Madeleine with admiration.

"Thank you! And congratulations for winning the Long Pony Race last summer."

"Oh, that was a long time ago!" Fia laughed, and gave Blue Sham a pat in recognition of his victory.

Tomorrow would be the last day of the pony trek, and now they were on their way to their final stop before returning home.

George and Fia were riding side by side behind the others.

"We're staying out in the open tonight, near Mill Lake—we won't have far to go from there to get home," said George.

"Let's hope we won't be eaten up by mosquitoes," replied Fia.

She was anxious to get back to Lakeholme. All the time her thoughts had been with Tiny . . .

"George . . ."

"Yes?"

Fia looked away from him as she continued ". . . I rode Tiny that evening. Perhaps it's my fault if he's worse."

There was silence for some time. George looked at Fia and realized that she was very upset.

"Don't worry," he said. "I'm sure he'll be all right."

Fia and George caught up with the others and, pushing through thick bushes, the riders disappeared into the cool forest.

It was evening when they reached Mill Lake. In silence, they all rode across the shallow bay and up the slope toward the edge of the forest on the other side. That was where they would spend the night. The ponies were cared for and soon a campfire was burning beside the lake. George and the girls gathered near the flames. It was a calm, windless evening.

Fia checked that everything was in order at the camp site. When this was done, she walked toward the flames which seemed to dance between the tree trunks. When she was halfway there, she stopped in her tracks. They were talking about Tiny.

"How is Tiny getting along, really, George?" asked one of the girls. George didn't have time to answer before Karin broke in.

"Is it really dangerous for a horse to eat too much?"

"Yes, it can be bad," explained George. "It can set up poisoning which in time affects the hoofs and, in really bad cases, it can make the horse permanently lame."

For a moment Fia felt paralyzed with fright.

"Permanently lame"—it couldn't happen—not to Tiny.

She pulled herself together and walked down to the others.

"Let's sing," suggested Eva.

They all joined in—except Fia. She stared into the fire. More than anything she wanted to saddle Pontus and ride quickly home to Tiny.

She wanted to know, one way or another . . .

Carefully, George put the fire out. The girls settled down for the night.

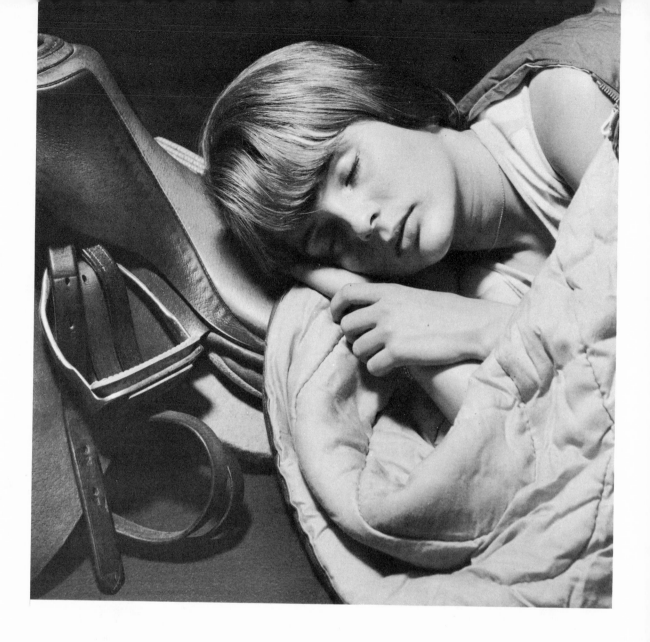

Fia crept into her sleeping bag and adjusted the saddle under her head. She found it difficult to go to sleep. She watched the moonbeams filtering through the branches and listened to all the sounds of the night. She tried to rid herself of the feeling of impending disaster.

At last she dropped off into a restless sleep.

The wind swept like a sigh through the forest, bringing with it the scent of pine needles and resin. On the valley floor the mists enveloped the scenery in a thousand veils.

Fia had bad dreams . . . about Tiny. It seemed to her that he was in danger, and that he was calling for her . . .

She woke with a start and leaned on her elbow. Had she dreamed it all, or had she heard Tiny cry?

She looked around. All the other girls were asleep. Fia felt very uneasy. Then she heard the cry again.

She looked up, and in the moonlight she saw a great ghostlike shadow cross the sky.

"What was that?" asked Christine, startled out of her sleep.

"I don't know, a bird perhaps . . ."

"It sounded strange," said Eva, who had also awakened.

Now Fia knew what she must do. The feeling of coming disaster still had her in its grip. She must ride home—now, at once!

She woke George.

"I want to go home."

"Now? In the middle of the night?"

"I have a feeling that Tiny is in danger."

"All right, if that's what you want to do. But take one or two of the girls with you—you shouldn't ride alone."

"Christine and Eva are awake—they can come with me."

George gave a sigh, turned over, and went to sleep again.

Like three phantom riders the girls left the camp.

They rode up the ridge, then carefully made their way by moonlight down the other side. In the forest they followed what had once been a path but was now grown over, and reached a stream, winding its way between the trees.

"We will have to lead the horses here," said Fia, as she reined in Pontus. "We've got to cross this narrow bridge."

The girls dismounted and led the ponies across.

Silently they continued their journey into the dark forest.

The air was getting more oppressive, and black banks of clouds appeared on the horizon. There were a few fierce gusts of wind, and the moon disappeared. It was as if the whole countryside were holding its breath.

The first flash of lightning came without warning from straight above and struck the ground like a flaming white spear. Pontus reared, and Fia had trouble holding him in check. She spoke to him, but her voice was drowned in the ear-splitting crash which followed.

Fresh flashes of lightning crossed each other and streaked with a hiss into the forest ahead of them.

Fia caught up with the others.

"There's a barn over there," she yelled through the din of the thunder.

The next flash and the thunder both came together.

"It's exactly above us," shouted Eva, and her face was a deathly white as she turned toward Fia.

Hurriedly, the girls tied the ponies to trees and groped their way into the barn. Fia brushed away the cobwebs which clung to her face. The barn was dilapidated, and there was a pungent stale smell of dust and rotten straw.

"I'm frightened."

Eva held tightly on to Fia's arm and tried to hide behind Christine.

The great barn door creaked and banged to and fro in the wind, but there was no rain. Fia looked out. She saw a dead tree that, ghostlike, seemed to stretch its black arms toward the illuminated sky. On one of the branches she thought she could see a big, black bird of ill-omen. When the next flash pierced the air, it was gone . . .

When the storm was finally over, the girls saw daylight outside.

The girls tried to calm the ponies, who were uneasily sniffling the air. The sound of thunder could now be heard faintly in the distance—but Fia picked up another sound. At first she could not place it. But then the smell came to her nostrils. She hurled herself into the saddle and galloped up the hill. She looked out over the forest. Panic-stricken, she turned toward the others and shouted:

"THE FOREST IS ON FIRE!"

Toward the west Fia could see the flames dancing, rising toward the sky. The gusts of wind caused the fire to spread from tree to tree. Now and then, a muffled bang could be heard. It sounded as if the trees were exploding.

A stream of sparks rose toward the sky, coloring it red. The long drought had made the forest an easy prey to the flames. The fire was spreading with raging fury.

Christine and Eva rode up to the crest beside Fia. For a time they stood paralyzed, watching the fearful spectacle.

It was Christine who broke the silence. "Look over there!"

She shivered with horror as she pointed to the north.

Fia looked.

"It can't be true," she said slowly.

The whole forest seemed to be on fire. A blazing wall of flame rose toward the sky, throwing out blackish-gray smoke and darkening the sky.

Fia was horrified.

"Over there, on the other side of the hill, is the big paddock—it won't be long before the fire gets to it . . ."

". . . and the big paddock is full of ponies," continued Eva, looking at Christine.

Fia thought quickly. "There's still a chance to get to the paddock before the fire!"

"We've got to do something! Christine, ride back to warn George and the girls. They must go home another way. And you, Eva, ride to Norrgarden—they've got a telephone there. Call the fire department and then call Lakeholme. I'm going to try to get to the paddock."

"You can't," pleaded Eva. "It's not safe."

"I must . . . for the sake of the horses."

Fia wheeled Pontus around and rode off. Nothing could stop her!

The girls watched her as she went.

"We've got to hurry." Christine was firm. "You know the way to Norrgarden, don't you?"

"Oh yes," replied Eva, gathering up the reins and urging her pony into motion.

"But be careful!" called Christine.

Christine gave the spreading fire a last glance.

"I hope Fia gets there in time," she thought.

Then she turned and rode downhill. She had decided she would cross the inlet. That way she would gain a lot of time.

Slowly she rode across the stony edge of the lake, looking for a good place to cross. She was in a hurry, but she could take no risks.

There were some boulders blocking her way, and she had to leave the edge of the lake in order to pass them. Then she spotted the derelict pier projecting out into the water.

"Wait here," she said to her pony, Stella, as she dismounted.

As if on a tightrope she walked along the pier, balancing herself on the crumbling boards, and looked into the water. The bottom was covered with seaweed, but it seemed to be free of rocks. She returned to Stella.

"We'll try this place . . ." she said to her pony as she mounted and let Stella step slowly into the water. "That's right, only just a little farther, then we'll swim."

But Stella lost her foothold. She tried again to find her feet, but slid on a slippery stone. She got scared and shied.

"Steady!" called Christine quietly.

But Stella was frightened. She wanted to escape from all the perils which lurked below the water. She kicked, and Christine slipped sideways.

Trying to regain her balance, she pushed her foot hard into the left stirrup, and in a cascade of water both Christine and the saddle plunged in. The girth straps had broken!

When Christine came to the surface, she lifted the soaking wet saddle, took Stella by the bridle, and led her back to the shore.

"We must find another way."

Meanwhile, Fia had skirted the edge of the suffocating wall of smoke. She could feel the heat from the raging fire getting fiercer. By the old stone quarry she turned into the dried-out river bed which she followed until she reached the stream. Then, sheltered by an outcropping of rock, she rode to the north side of the paddock.

Now she could hear the sound of thundering hoofs and wild cries from the enclosure. Suddenly her path was blocked by flames. The undergrowth was on fire!

"We haven't time to go around. We've got to ride through it!" she said aloud.

Fia held Pontus in and patted him reassuringly. He backed a few paces, tossed his head, and snorted.

"Now it all depends on you . . ." Fia told him.

She took a firmer grip on the reins. Then she closed her legs firmly and rode straight into the smoke.

Fia's eyes smarted and she coughed. But she and Pontus made it! Now she could see the enclosure and the ponies, their backs soaking with perspiration and their manes flying as they galloped in wild panic. Terrified neighs pierced the air. At times a cloud of smoke enveloped them.

Fia paused. Then she opened the big gate and rode in. She had no idea what she was going to do when suddenly the ponies appeared out of the smoke. She saw their wild eyes and dilated nostrils as, led by the black stallion, they hurtled straight toward her.

There was no way of stopping the wildly rushing herd and, fearfully, Fia watched the ponies stampede toward her.

All at once the stallion changed direction, and the rest followed him. In a moment they had all thundered through the open gate, smashing the posts with their iron-shod feet. As the ponies pressed through, one of them fell from exhaustion.

Fia felt weak. She and Pontus stood alone in the paddock. She seemed still to hear the thunder of hoofs and to see the herd rush toward her.

"They're safe now," she said, and led Pontus out through the smashed gateway.

She got into the saddle and rode off. The raging fire and the intense heat were behind her. She rode down toward Stone Lake.

Fia felt dizzy and confused. When she reached the lake she found it was easier to breathe. Pontus drank eagerly, and Fia splashed her face with the cool water.

Now she had to come to a decision—about Tiny.

Either he was still in the small paddock in the woods, and it wouldn't be long before the fire reached it . . . or he stood safely at home in the stable. But if she rode home, and he was not there . . . she would never get back to the paddock in time. The fire would be there before her . . .

That decided her. If she crossed the water she would gain time and be able to reach the paddock before the fire.

"We're going for a swim," she said to Pontus.

She mounted and rode into the shallows. When Pontus was out of his depth, Fia slipped out of the saddle. She gripped his mane and, keeping by his side, guided him toward the other shore.

"Oh, I hope Christine and Eva managed all right, and that the poor frightened ponies from the big paddock have calmed down," she said, patting Pontus' neck.

Pontus snorted in reply.

Slowly and cautiously, Fia climbed the shore and followed a well-trodden forest path. Again she smelled the smoke in the wind. She made her way through the thicket. Branches whipped her in the face, and the bushes swept Pontus' sides.

She pressed on through the forest, her eyes smarting. Then she caught sight of the thatched roof of the unused farmhouse. She tied Pontus to a tree and climbed the fence.

The smoke came in gusts, and she found it hard to breathe. She called Tiny's name, stopped and listened. Then she thought she could hear a neigh in the distance. She felt her way in the direction of the sound, tripping over roots and scratching her hands on the briars.

Step by step she penetrated into the thicket.

The smoke came in waves, pricking and hot.

Her eyes smarted when she tried to see through the smoke.

Then she heard it plainly!

Somewhere in there was a horse, uttering terrified neighs. Tiny? Fia forgot the danger. The smoke came at her from all sides and half-blinded her. The sounds of a forest, exploding with fire, came ever nearer.

She hesitated—but only for an instant. She had to go on—Tiny's life was at stake!

Then she saw a misty form in the thick smoke. She stopped and bent near the ground to see better. Was it her imagination? Or did she faintly see a light-colored shape moving behind two boulders? She held her breath . . . then the shape rose . . . and gave an anguished neigh!

IT WAS TINY!

Fia crawled under a fallen tree trunk and ran the last few steps toward him.

"Tiny!"

Her voice broke as she shouted his name.

Tiny saw something coming toward him. He was frightened out of his wits and looked on this as a fresh danger. In front of him there were two boulders and, on each side, fallen trees, whose sharp branches had gashed his quarters. Behind him was the fire and the heat. He was surrounded . . .

Petrified with fear, he stared at this thing which was rushing toward him. He reared and struck out with his forelegs.

Fia did everything she could to calm him—but in vain. The roar ahead of her grew louder. She felt helpless . . . and ready to burst into tears.

Blinded by smoke, gasping for air, torn by branches and scrub, Fia experienced it all as a nightmare. She was ready to drop from exhaustion.

"I can't save you, Tiny!"

Then she collected her thoughts.

"Tiny! Tiny! I'll be back."

Desperate, she hurried away. She fell headlong over a crumbling tree trunk. Her leg felt painful, but she had to go on . . . had to return before the raging inferno reached the paddock and Tiny, as it must before long.

Panting from exertion, she arrived at the farm. The door of the old barn hung by a rusty hinge. She tore open the door, and there on the wall she found what she had come for . . . a long coil of rope. Swiftly she made a loop, and the rope became a lasso.

She heard Tiny cry with fear. She was dead tired, but the sound from the forest, which was burning like a thousand torches, made her return.

There he was again, rearing, terrified, backing away from the boulders, but not daring to back farther because of all the strange sounds which filled the forest.

Fia was close. Again she tried to calm Tiny, but he was frantic with fear. "Tiny! It's me . . . I want to help . . ."

She tried to get near him from behind. But he was on his guard.

Then, at last! The loop flew through the air, over Tiny's head, and settled high around his neck. Slowly, Fia approached.

Fia held him firmly and spoke reassuringly.

"There, there, I am here—Fia!"

It seemed almost as if Tiny recognized her.

"Come along, Tiny, steady now . . . it'll be over soon . . ."

She led him carefully, talking soothingly all the while, back to safety.

When she reached the farm, she threw her arms around Tiny's neck and wept.

From a nearby tree came a snort which made her turn around. Pontus was tugging and pulling to free himself.

Fia led Tiny and untied Pontus. He was throwing his head about. He kicked and tried to tear himself away from her hold. Fia did her best to hold both ponies, but she knew she couldn't last much longer.

Then she heard voices, and out of the smoke came some of the girls from Lakeholme on their ponies.

"There she is! I knew she would be here."

Harriet, on the first pony, jumped from her saddle and came rushing forward.

"Are you hurt?" she asked, looking anxiously at Fia.

"I'm all right, but I couldn't have gone on much longer . . ."

Harriet glanced quickly at the forest and the red flames licking the trunks.

"We've got to get away from here. Saddle Tiny! He's all right now," she went on, turning to Fia. "Take Pontus' saddle . . ."

As Fia listened to Harriet's voice, she became perfectly calm.

"Hurry!" Harriet urged, helping Fia into the saddle. "There'll be fire all around us if we don't get away fast. Follow me . . ."

"How did you know that I was here?" asked Fia when they were safe.

"It was Eva. She called the fire department and us. We were on our way to the big paddock when we met ponies in the valley. I knew it was you who had managed to save them—and I knew that Tiny was still in the small paddock. After that, is wasn't difficult to figure out where you were."

Harriet gazed at Fia's blackened face, streaked with tears.

"You should take a look at yourself!" she said.

When the girls were halfway home, the rain came. After weeks and weeks of drought, the skies opened, and torrents of water gushed over the thirsty countryside.

The firemen worked feverishly. The rain did its part, and the fire never reached farther than to the firebreak, which is the wide avenue designed to stop the spread of forest fires.

All the ponies were rounded up, and toward evening they were taken home. Fia saw them come up the hill, silhouetted against the rose-tinted sky. The storm and the rain had cleansed the air. It was cooler now.

The day when the forest caught fire was nearing its close.

Fia tried to collect her thoughts. She had made her way to the quiet living room to be alone. She felt as if she had just awakened and that all the terrors of the time in the forest during the last few hours were only a dream. She closed her eyes, but still she saw Tiny in her mind's eye, tossing his head in panic.

She looked out of the window.

George came walking across the courtyard. She heard the creaking of the floorboards, and the massive door groaned on its hinges as he opened it and stepped inside.

Quietly, Fia turned around.

George looked at her with admiration as he went over to shake her hand.

"Thank you, Fia, for all you've done!"

After that there was silence for some time.

Then they heard a whinny from somewhere outside.

"Take a look, Fia!"

She turned, and George opened the window wide.

Out there stood George's father, and he was holding Tiny's reins. Behind him in a wide circle stood the girls: Harriet, Karin, Christine, Eva, and all the others.

Tiny was pawing the ground with his hoof.

"Come on out, Fia!"

The Captain didn't sound quite as stern as usual.

"We would like to thank you—and to give you a present which you richly deserve."

Fia felt herself turning as red as a beet.

Then she rushed out through the door . . .